THE EVENT

DALLENT

MIKE THIS **SHIT REALLY** FREAKS ME OUT!

IT **FREAKS** ME OUT **TOO,** MALCOLM, BUT I HAVE TO **KNOW** WHAT SHE'S UP TO.

I'M NOT **TALKING** ABOUT **DARCI,** MIKE. I'M **REFERRING** TO THE **PORTRAIT.**

IT'S JUST SOME **STUDENTS FOOLING** AROUND.

DARCI SAYS IT **HAPPENS** ALL THE **TIME** AROUND HERE.

WE'VE **GOT** TO TURN IT BACK AROUND.

YOU **KNOW** HOW I AM, MIKE.

IT'LL **BOTHER** ME THE **REST** OF THE **DAY,** IF WE **DON'T.**

WE **DON'T** HAVE **TIME** FOR **THIS.**

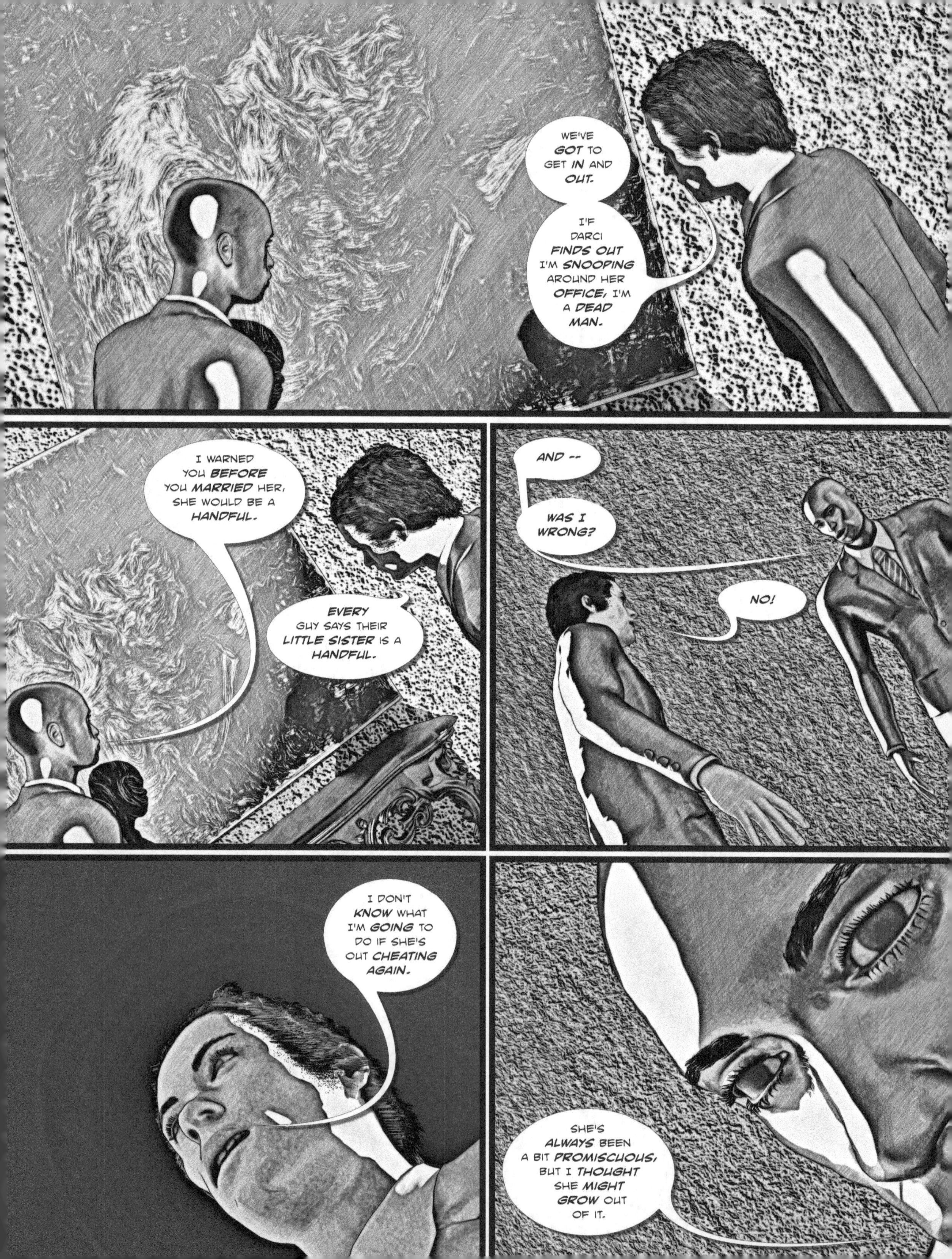

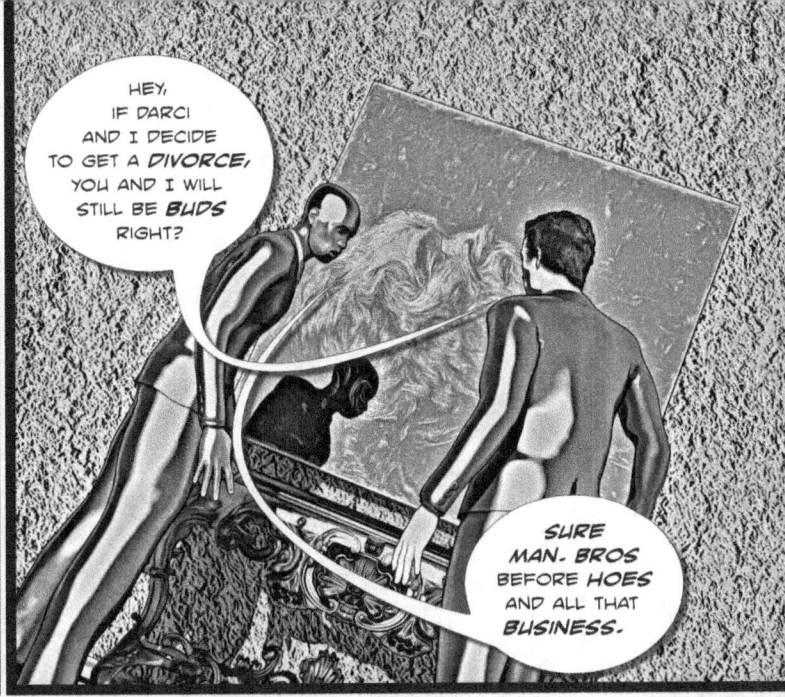

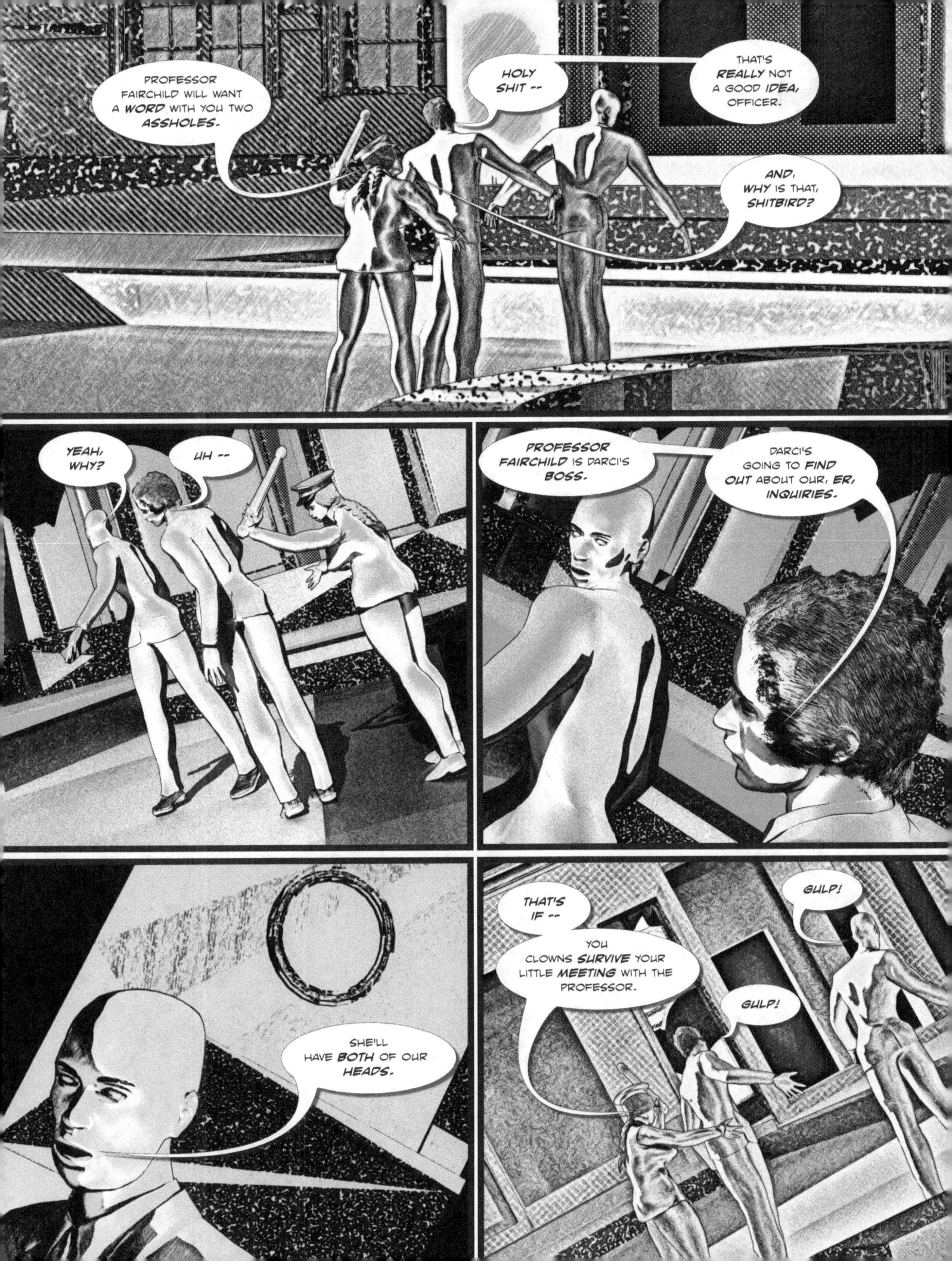

WELL, I THINK *HATE* IS A *STRONG WORD,* CODY.

LET'S JUST *SAY* WE'RE *STRUGGLING* A *BIT* WITH THE *SEX* PART OF THE *RELATIONSHIP.*

THIS IS *ALL VERY INTERESTING,* BUT LADIES IF WE DON'T GET THE *HELL OUT* OF *HERE* . . .

OH, I *SEE.* SOME *BAD MEN* ARE GOING TO TAKE US *PRISONER* AND *FUCK* US INTO *NEXT* SUNDAY.

ONLY IF WE'RE *REALLY* LUCKY.

THINGS CAN GO *DARK* PRETTY *QUICKLY* IN *SOME* DOMAINS.

FLEDGLINGS!

IT *SURE* SEEMS LIKE WE'RE *TAKING* THE *LONG* WAY AROUND.

WHOA, THIS PLACE IS LIKE A MAZE!
LIKE A MAZE?
Risk Pool
THINGS HAVE CHANGED SINCE LAST I WAS HERE.
I CONFESS THAT I MIGHT BE JUST A BIT TURNED AROUND.
WONDERFUL?
Risk Pool
Risk Pool
WHOEVER NOW OWNS THIS DOMAIN HAS MADE SOME CHANGES.
THE FIRST THING THE DOM USUALLY DOES IS HIDE THE EXIT.
Risk Pool
I'M NOT SURE WHY THEY'VE MADE IS SO DIFFICULT FOR US TO GET TO THE PARTY.
IT SEEMS LIKE WILLING WOMEN WOULD BE WHAT YOU'D WANT AT A KINKY SEX PARTY.
HAH!
THEY WON'T WANT US TO MOVE ON FOR THE REASONS YOU JUST MENTIONED.
WE'D BE FORCED TO NEGOTIATE TO GAIN ACCESS TO THE EXIT PORTAL.
WILLING MY ASS. THAT DAMN PROFESSOR FAIRCHILD BLACKMAILED ME INTO COMING HERE.
AND -- I DON'T QUITE GET THE WHOLE COMPETITION ANGLE?

ACACIA, BRING ME MY STRAPON!

IT WOULD BE A *PLEASURE*, MISTRESS.

TAKE IT FROM ME, YOU ASSHOLES AREN'T GOING TO LIKE THIS SHIT!

NOW WAIT JUST A *DAMN* MINUTE.

STUFF LIKE *CROOKED ART FREAKS* MALCOLM *OUT.*

WE WERE JUST *RETURNING* THAT *PORTRAIT* TO IT'S ORIGINAL POSITION.

HAH, LIKELY STORY!

DON'T *BELIEVE* A *WORD* THEY SAY, MISTRESS, *ER,* PROFESSOR.

www.ingramcontent.com/pod-product-compliance
Lightning Source LLC
Chambersburg PA
CBHW082018170626
46817CB00009B/3132